The Junior Novel
Adapted by Alice Alfonsi
Based on the Disney Channel Original Movie,
"Cheetah Girls 2", written by Felicia Henderson and Alison Taylor
Based upon the series of books by Deborah Gregory

New York

Printed in the United States of America

First Edition
1 3 5 7 9 10 8 6 4 2

Library of Congress Control Number: 2005908222

ISBN: 1-4231-0080-8

For more Disney Press fun, visit www.disneybooks.com
Visit DisneyChannel.com

1

Manhattan Magnet's auditorium was a party paradise. Balloons bobbed along the ceiling, and confetti rained down like Technicolor snow. Hanging from the rafters, a banner proclaimed, CONGRATS GRADS! WELCOME TO THE JUNGLE! But nobody was looking at the decorations. All eyes were on the empty stage.

"Cheetahs! Cheetahs!" cheered the crowd.

The students whistled and whooped. They wanted an encore!

In the wings, the four Cheetahs couldn't believe their ears. Their last number had a bass line so tight they were still catching their breaths. And the crowd wanted *more*?!

Galleria's big brown eyes flashed with pride. Two years ago, the Cheetahs had been the first freshmen ever to win the high school's talent contest. Now they were wise old juniors—hotter than ever and *always* ready to play.

And that's exactly what they did. The four fierce felines slapped hands, curled their claws in a pounding shake, and pounced right back into the spotlight!

When the audience saw the Cheetahs reappear, their shouts shook the building. And when they heard the first notes of "The

Party's Just Begun," the applause got even louder.

The Cheetah Girls' voices were pure, and their dance moves were slammin'. Soon everyone was singing, clapping, and getting automatically amped by the Cheetah rhythms.

The girls had so much growl power, their hearts were still pumping after they fled the stage. Friends and classmates followed them into the gym's locker room, showering them with flowers and props.

The Cheetahs chatted with their fans until they were exhausted. Then, Galleria politely ushered the bubbly group out the door.

Finally getting a moment's peace, the girls slumped together on a locker room bench. After some deep breathing, they began to change back into their street clothes.

"We made it," Galleria declared. "Junior year is over like a four-leaf clover!"

Galleria "Bubbles" Garibaldi was the

Cheetah Girls' songwriter and founder. Her sleek, uptown style was in her DNA. (Her mom was a former international fashion model. And her dad was from Bologna—not full of it.)

"Y'all are my girls," said Aqua, "but I still miss Houston."

"Darling Cheetah!" shrieked Galleria, striking a drama queen pose. "When you go back, Houston will be throwing you the Aqua Days parade!"

Aqua laughed. "The Aqua Days parade *and barbecue*," she declared, practicing her royal wave. "I like it!"

Tall and slender, Aquanette Walker was all Texas flava. She had a powerhouse voice, plenty of sassy cowgirl attitude, and her grin was as big as her home state. She was also a whiz at all things bookish, which is why her nickname was "Einstein-ette."

Chanel "Chuchie" Simmons, on the other hand, was trendy and girly with a spicy flair, just like her Latina mom. Back in the day, Chanel's mother had modeled with Galleria's mother. That was why Chanel had been down with Galleria's growl power forever— or at least since they'd been divettes in diapers.

Unfortunately, despite the Cheetah credo to spend more time on your homework than your hair, schoolwork was not one of Chuchie's favorite things.

"I thought we were going to have to box around SAT time," she said, flipping her wavy brown hair. "I'm not going to lie. You tied me to the chair."

"And you got the big 1800, didn't you?" Dorinda asked.

Dó Re Mi was the Cheetah's best dancer and the group's choreographer. Street-smart, with a funky rock-star style, she lived with foster parents and ten other foster children in the basement of an apartment building. Money was tight in the Bosco house, so when it came to schoolwork, Dó wasn't playing. She worked hard for her grades—like she worked hard for *everything*.

"NYU can't say no to the Cheetahs!" Galleria exclaimed.

"And it's finally summer," Dorinda pointed out. "Maybe we can rest a little."

Galleria shot the girl a look before she even finished her sentence.

"Or not . . ." Dorinda amended with a shrug.

Later, while Dó and Aqua talked with some friends who'd come to the concert, Galleria and Chanel sat down with their mothers.

Galleria announced, "I've already mapped out the summer rehearsal schedule."

Chanel rolled her eyes. "Remember when she was a control freak? She's much better now."

Galleria bristled. *Snap!* she thought. My

Cheetah sisters already set me straight on the whole "you're not the boss of me" score. But every so often *someone's* got to light the way!

"All I'm saying is we should stay sharp until we book some gigs for the summer," Galleria argued.

"We're visiting my cousins on Martha's Vineyard in a few weeks," said Dorothea, Galleria's mom.

"The Vineyard is perfect!" Galleria cried, immediately revising her Cheetah plan. "Lots of fancy people there. *Producer* people."

Dorothea frowned. She hadn't been a model in years. (These days she ran a store called Toto . . . Fun in Diva Sizes and sold her own small handbag line.) But she was still a class-A diva—tall, elegant, and totally intimidating when she wanted to be. Like *now*.

"Galleria, we're going to have some family time this summer," she said. "And you'll have to give the singing a rest when they go to Barcelona."

Chanel's mother, Juanita, tensed. She threw Dorothea a look.

"When *who* goes to Barcelona?" Chanel asked.

Dorothea turned to Juanita. "You told me not to mention something tonight, right?" she quietly asked. "Was it this? Or the part about you getting a tattoo?"

Chanel couldn't believe her ears. Her mother was ultratrendy, strikingly beautiful, and had more Cheetah-licious clothes than the display floor of Saks Fifth Avenue. But some days, she acted more like a sister than a mother. That made them best friends on good days, but bickering siblings on bad ones. And Chanel could see it was about to become a bad one.

"Tattoo? Of what? Something corny like a butterfly? A unicorn?" Screaming with laughter, Galleria rolled across Chanel's bed.

"Can we focus?" Chanel snapped, pacing barefoot across her bedroom carpet. "Now I have to hang around Spain with her and her boyfriend?"

Chanel's mom and dad had been divorced for a few years now. *That* Chanel was okay with. What she wasn't okay with was her mother's boyfriend, Luc.

"They've been dating for a long time," Galleria pointed out. "Is this a surprise?"

Chanel stopped pacing and threw up her hands. "If he was going to propose, he would have by now. She looks desperate. It's embarrassing."

Galleria's brow wrinkled. "It's a free trip to Spain. What's this really about?"

"If my mom gets married to Luc, she's going to want me to move there so she can have a new family." Chanel sighed and sunk down on her mattress.

"Chuchie, I don't know how we're going to fix this, but no one is going to break us up. I promise." Galleria put an arm around her oldest friend and gave her a hug.

"I've seen all these dresses before. Nothing extraordinaire," Dorothea said as she flipped through the glossy pages of a bridal magazine.

While Galleria and Chanel talked in the bedroom, their mothers were looking at wedding dresses in the living room.

Juanita sighed. "That's why, when the time comes, you have to design my gown."

"You're sweet," replied Dorothea. "But those days are long gone."

Juanita shrugged. "First things first. I need the ring."

"Mom," Chanel called as she walked into the room, "I gave myself an attitude check."

Juanita faced her daughter.

"I'm down for going to Spain, and spending time with . . ." Chanel had to force herself to get the dreaded name past her lips. "Luc."

"*Gracias, mija,*" Juanita replied, giving her daughter a hug. "I appreciate that."

"It's important to you, so I'll make it work. I'm really gonna miss my girls though," Chanel admitted.

"I know. It's only going to be a month, honey," said Juanita.

"If we can work out the flights and the money and everything, can the Cheetahs come with us?" Chanel asked. Dorothea and Juanita couldn't see that Galleria was right outside the door, encouraging Chanel to keep trying.

But Dorothea smelled something fishy— with Cheetah spots. "Did Galleria put you up to this?" she asked.

"No, *Madrina*," said Chanel, who liked to use the spanish word for godmother when talking to her *own* godmother, Dorothea. "I just thought, there's plenty of room, and . . ."

"We're leaving in three days," said Juanita. "It's too late to ask Luc to host more people. It would be rude. There'll be other times . . . hopefully."

As Juanita smiled at her, Chanel just stood there feeling defeated. The Cheetahs wouldn't be going to Spain. Not now. Maybe not ever. *Nunca*.

3

The next night, the Cheetahs assembled in Galleria's bedroom. Between mouthfuls of take-out Chinese dumplings and spicy kung pao chicken, the girls discussed their *persuasion* problem. When they got down to the oranges and fortune cookies, Chanel pushed aside her plate and chopsticks, and plunked her backpack on the table. Hoping to inspire her sisters, she pulled out a pile of Spanish magazines.

"Awwww, Barcelona is so crazy beautiful. I can't believe we're not going," Galleria exclaimed.

"I know," Aqua said wistfully. "I've loved Spain and its history and its people ever since my first Enrique Iglesias concert."

"I've tried everything," said Chanel. "She won't budge."

Galleria closed the magazine and thought for a moment. "If the Cheetahs have to be on pause for a second, what would we do this summer?"

"There's a kids' dance camp that wants me to teach. More baby-sitting, really." Dorinda shrugged.

Aqua drummed her fingers. "You know those biology classes I take at Columbia? My professor's doing research on structures of membrane proteins at atomic resolution. I guess I could glom onto that . . ."

The Cheetahs stared speechless. Then

Dorinda turned to Aqua. "Who are you sometimes?"

Just then, Aqua turned to look out the window. "Oh, my gosh," she screamed in amazement. "There's a shooting star! Wish!"

Galleria, Dorinda, and Chanel all closed their eyes, crossed their fingers, and wished. They needed *something* to help them get to Spain. Why not a shooting star? "Barcelona!" they cried in unison.

Hoping their wish would come true, the girls turned back to their magazines.

"Chuchie, what does this say?" Galleria asked as she pointed to an ad.

Chanel leaned in closer, her eyes widening. "It's an ad for the Barcelona Summer Music Festival. And it features a New Voices competition for undiscovered talent!"

Galleria didn't waste a second. She took the magazine over to her computer and started typing.

When the festival's Web site appeared on

the screen, Chanel translated. "All ages welcome. Apply here by . . ." Chanel's face fell suddenly. She could hardly stand to tell the others the bad news. "The deadline was last week."

"Deadline, schmedline," Galleria replied with determination. She whipped out her cell phone. "Here's the number."

With hope in their eyes, Dorinda, Aqua, and Chanel watched Galleria call across the Atlantic.

"We'll call these people, tell them who we are," Galleria babbled, "and we'll . . ." She listened for a second, then checked her watch. "Get back with them when it's not four in the morning over there."

Hours later, the Cheetahs were sprawled all over Galleria's bedroom, snoring away until—

Ting-ting! Ting-ting! Ting-ting!

Galleria snapped awake at the very first *Ting!* of her cell phone alarm. Okay, she thought, this Cheetah's awake and ready to pounce!

She grabbed her phone and dialed at the speed of light. "Hello?" she said when she heard a voice on the other end. "Is this the . . . hello? One moment, *uno momento por favor* . . ."

"Chuchie!" she called. But Chanel was still in dreamland. Galleria raced across the room and yanked one of the girl's braids. "Chanel, wake up!"

"Ow! What?!" Chanel groused.

"Chanel!" Galleria shoved the phone into her friend's hand. "Spain is awake. Talk to them!"

As Chanel yawned and introduced herself in Spanish, Galleria shook Aqua and Dorinda. "Guys!"

"What? . . . What's happening?" the two muttered, rubbing their eyes.

Galleria's hands fluttered wildly. "Chanel is talking to the festival!"

Chanel frowned and covered the phone. "She's saying we're too late. She says apply for next year."

"Bump next year! We could *win* that contest now! They're gonna miss out on this?" Galleria grabbed the phone and held it up like a microphone. Then she gathered the girls around and started singing "Cheetah Sisters". The others got a clue and quickly began to harmonize.

Their sound was tight and gorgeous—soft enough to keep from waking Galleria's mom but sweet enough (they hoped!) to reach across the Atlantic and charm their skeptical audience of one.

When the song was over, Chanel put the phone to her ear again. "Señora?" she asked timidly, hoping Spain was still on the line.

The Cheetahs held their breath. Finally, a

grin dawned on Chuchie's face from ear to ear!

"She said download the application, have it signed, and we have an appointment with the festival director next week!" Chanel cried after finishing the call and hanging up.

The girls jumped up and down, screaming *silently*—because they hadn't forgotten about Dorothea sleeping in the next room.

"If we are really going to make this happen," Galleria said excitedly, "then we have to promise each other that when we get to Barcelona, we will focus, work hard, and do our best to win. Then no one and nothing can break us apart!"

That evening, Dorothea sat next to Juanita in the Garibaldis' well-appointed living room. As the two mothers sipped tea, they listened to the Cheetahs make their pitch.

". . . we'll arrange for you and Luc to have front row seats at the Barcelona Summer Music Festival. The biggest festival in Europe!" Galleria exclaimed.

"Oh, don't spend your money on us, girls," said Juanita.

"It's free, Mom. Because the Cheetah Girls are singing in the New Voices competition at the festival!" Chanel could barely contain her excitement.

"You're in the music festival?" Juanita asked.

"We saw the ad last night. We called them and auditioned over the phone," explained Chanel.

"Just like that?" Dorothea said, skeptical but impressed by the girls' ingenuity.

"The universe is clearly at work here," said Galleria. "In fact, I'm afraid *not* to go. Do you want to mess with the plans of the universe? I don't."

Dorothea tossed Chanel's mother a dubious look. "Did you hear that, Juana? The whole universe is involved."

"It's an amazing opportunity, Mom," Chanel added. "So many artists have been discovered there. And since Luc's got plenty of room . . ."

"All we have to do is get there. And Daddy says—"

"You called your father in Hong Kong to talk about this?" Dorothea interrupted with a frown.

Galleria nodded. "He offered me and Dó his airline miles, so the trip is almost free."

"Is your foster mother all right with this, Dorinda?" Juanita asked.

"All right with a chance for me to go to Europe?" Dorinda held up her bulging backpack. "I'm packed!"

Everyone laughed, then Aqua spoke up. "My father made a list of the souvenirs he wants, but I told him I'm not going into the import/export business. I mean, that is—"

She glanced meaningfully at Juanita. "—if we're *allowed* to go."

"This is a special trip for you, Mom," pleaded Chanel. "It might change your life. Now it might change all of our lives. Please."

Juanita threw up her hands in surrender. "You've got to come with us, Dorothea. I don't think I can handle them alone."

As the girls hollered for joy, Dorothea stood and gathered the empty teacups. Tapping Galleria's shoulder, she motioned for her to come into the kitchen.

Galleria chewed her lip as she followed her mother. "Are you mad, Mom?" she asked.

The girls were still whooping it up in the next room as Dorothea shook her head. "Galleria Garibaldi. An international music contest? You'll be on your way back home if there's any monkey business," said Dorothea. "When vacation is over, you come home and focus on college."

Galleria didn't miss a beat. "Winning this

contest can only help for college. And we can defer a year if we have to go on tour."

Dorothea's eyebrows rose in surprise. *Checkmate*, she thought. My little girl is definitely not a Cheetah cub anymore.

"I'm just saying . . ." Galleria told her mom with a shrug.

"No, *I'm* just saying," Dorothea replied, trying to maintain a firm tone.

But both mother and daughter knew they'd gotten through to each other, and they broke their stubborn stares with a laugh.

"Let's pack!" Galleria said, hugging her mom.

A few days later, the Cheetahs and their mothers were walking toward the entrance of New York's John F. Kennedy airport.

"I hope Toto forgives us for leaving him in the kennel," Galleria said sadly.

"We'll call his personal tummy scratcher every day to check on him," Dorothea said reassuringly.

Grinning, Galleria gestured to the door. "Cheetahs, when we walk in this door, we are no longer American divas-in-training," she declared. "We're international superstars-in-training. Who's ready?"

After glancing at each other, the Cheetahs grabbed hands. Then four very different girls pounced into the air with one shared thought: hola, *Barcelona! Here we come!*

4

❖ ❖ ❖ ❖ ❖ ❖ ❖ ❖ ❖ ❖ ❖ ❖ ❖ ❖ ❖ ❖ ❖ ❖

"Ahhh . . . Las Ramblas," Chanel gushed, "the most fabulous street in Barcelona." She plopped down next to the other Cheetahs. They sat together near a marble fountain in a sunny, crowded square.

Dorinda pulled off her sunglasses and tilted her head back until the fountain's cool spray kissed her face. Not far away, the melodious sound of cathedral bells echoed through the colorful streets lined with rustic stone buildings that were centuries old.

"The Cheetahs are reigning in Spain," Dó declared with a sigh.

The Cheetahs had been exploring Las Ramblas, a wide, tree-lined boulevard that ran through the center of Barcelona from the Harbor to Catalunya Square. The legendary street was bordered with cafés, art galleries, boutiques, and market stalls selling every-thing from fruits and flowers to clothing and crafts.

Dorinda read in her guidebook that Las Ramblas was considered the heart and soul of Barcelona, and she could believe it. Here, tourists from around the world mingled with the locals.

No cars were allowed, so people walked or rode bicycles and scooters. Dorinda even spied a few boys on boards and Rollerblades—very *hot* boys.

Along the way, they saw some wild sights,

too, like human statues standing around motionless. These were live people, costumed to resemble famous figures, then painted gold or silver or gray like stone.

"I've got to see that Sagrada Familia Cathedral," Aqua said. She read from her guidebook. "Antonio Gaudi, the most famous architect in all of Spain, started it in 1882 and isn't finished yet. And I thought I was slow."

Chanel winced at her friend's mangling of the language. "*Sa-grrada. Sa-grrada*," Chanel instructed. "You got an A in Spanish, but you flunked rolling your r's."

"I'm trrrrying," Aqua practiced as she flipped through her Barcelona guide. "Wait! The book says, 'For anyone who drinks from this fountain, there's a promise of love'," Aqua cried.

Galleria clapped her hands. "Government sponsored love-water! What a country!"

Laughing, the Cheetahs headed off.

Suddenly, Dorinda made a face, like she'd forgotten something. "I'll catch up," she called. "I left my sunglasses. . . ." She hurried back to the fountain. But instead of going to the spot where they'd been sitting, she took a big gulp of water from the spigot beside the romance-promising plaque.

Smiling, Dó wiped her lips with the back of her hand. Then she slipped her sunglasses out of her pocket, put them on, and hurried to catch up to her friends.

The Cheetahs followed Las Ramblas until they couldn't walk any farther. They collapsed at a café, content to just sit and talk for a while.

"Barcelona in a day. I'm exhausted!" Dó exclaimed, flipping back her long, blond hair.

As the Cheetahs watched the crowds swirl around them, they soaked in the scenery. Finally, Galleria glanced at her watch and sighed. "We'd better get to the villa and settle in. This was supposed to be a 'stroll'."

"I'm in no hurry," said Chanel, frowning.

"What time is the car picking us up?" Aqua asked.

Galleria snorted. "Listen to you! 'The car'!"

Aqua shrugged. "It's easy to get used to."

Galleria and Aqua shared a Cheetah handshake on that one.

"This is so where we belong. Living the Cheetah credo," Galleria proclaimed.

Chanel nodded. "Mingling with the international crowd."

Aqua agreed. "Citizens of the *world*!"

"I'm afraid I'm going to say something wrong and look like a tourist," Dorinda confided.

As a waiter brought four small glasses of soda, Galleria waved her hand. "Darling! A Cheetah Girl could *never* look like a tourist." She took a sip of her soda, and handed it back to the waiter. "This is diet, right?" she asked.

"I need some ice, please. And two sugars? And a bunch of lemon wedges? And could you bring me the can?"

The waiter rolled his eyes as he hurried off.

"Like I said, Cheetah Girls could *never* look like tourists," Galleria repeated.

While the girls continued to talk, the strains of a Spanish guitar floated into the café.

"Shhh! What's that?" Aqua asked.

Just then, a handsome street performer appeared, strumming a classical guitar. As he began to sing, he locked eyes with Galleria and smiled.

"Is there any such thing as too perfect?" Galleria said, hypnotized by the seductive music and the dashing musician.

"I think he's a Gypsy," said Aqua. "That's a culture from India, actually, dating back to . . ."

"Later, Aqua," Galleria whispered, rapt in

the music. She turned to Chanel. "What's that song? What's he saying?"

The next thing they knew, the musician moved toward their table, singing and playing his guitar.

"Follow me and discover my Barcelona," said Chanel, who was translating the lyrics so the other Cheetahs would understand.

"Thanks, but we're exhausted," said Galleria.

"We couldn't take another step," agreed Dorinda.

But Chanel couldn't help herself. "I'm not ready to see Luc. Come on, Cheetahs! When in Spain . . ."

Then the Cheetah Girls all stood and began to sing the same song—adding their own Cheetah-licious licks to the mix, of course!

Dancing out of the café and through the cobblestone lanes of the city, the Cheetahs brought the tune home with a bangin' finish.

When their song ended, the Cheetahs found themselves on an ancient stone bridge. Aqua, Chanel, and Dorinda hurried across. Galleria stayed on the bridge and whirled to face the stranger.

"Sorry," she said, "I never even got your name."

The man looped the guitar strap over his shoulder. "Angel," he whispered. "*Me llamo* Angel."

"Angel," Galleria repeated, looking sky-ward.

"*Sí*. Your name?"

"Galleria," she replied. "It means . . . um, a glamorous building where beautiful things are sold."

"Galleria," Angel said, making her name sound like poetry.

"Perfect." She sighed. "Thanks for sharing your Barcelona. It's beautiful."

From the other side of the bridge, Chanel called Galleria's name. The other Cheetahs were waiting next to a sleek black town car. A chauffeur in a tailored uniform held the door open for the girls.

Regretfully, Galleria said good-bye to Angel. Then she hurried to catch up with her girls.

5

By the time the Cheetahs' town car climbed through the Barcelona hills to Luc's home, the sun was close to setting. Late afternoon shadows descended as the vehicle rolled through a lush vineyard and orchard.

Finally, the car turned onto a cobblestone driveway, flanked by tall trees. When it stopped in the middle of a large courtyard, the chauffeur emerged and opened the door for the Cheetahs.

Chanel stepped out first. "*Gracias*, Señor Reynosa," she said, then waited for an introduction.

The dignified, gray-haired chauffeur bowed deeply. "*A sue ordenes*."

Chanel shook the man's hand, not sure if she felt right about having someone "at her service."

Behind Chanel, Aqua whistled. "I guess they don't make everything bigger in Texas."

Chanel frowned at the car parked in front of them. "Come on, girl. It's just a car."

"I don't mean that. I mean *that*!" Aqua pointed.

Chanel followed her friend's finger and gasped at the palace in front of them. The restored mansion was breathtaking in its size and beauty. But Villa Soler was the home of her mother's boyfriend. So she wasn't about to act impressed.

"Just another big old European villa, like you see in the movies," Chanel said with a dissing wave. "Act like you know, please."

An older woman in a long, black dress approached.

"My wife, Señora Reynosa," the chauffeur declared, by way of introduction.

"*Bienvenidos*, Señoritas Cheetahs," the woman said. "Welcome to Villa Soler."

The woman's smile relaxed them instantly. While the staff grabbed the girls' luggage, Señora Reynosa led them into the estate's magnificently restored carriage house, which now served as the villa's guest quarters.

The girls gaped at the house's main room. It had a high ceiling, tall windows, and a spectacular view of the sea in the distance. The room was filled with luxurious furnishings fit for a queen—or a Cheetah!

"These rooms were the former carriage house of the villa, which was built in 1888 by the Marquis of Soler," the señora said.

"Señor Luc has converted it to additional guest quarters so he can have all his friends and family around him. Everything is designed with your comfort in mind," Señora Reynosa continued. "Your bedrooms are through those doors. Breakfast is served in the garden at ten. Laundry baskets are in your rooms for nightly pick-up. Please see me for anything else you may require." Then the woman curtsied and turned to leave.

"Oh, Señora Reynosa?" Galleria called. "We might be in and out quite a bit. I'll be in charge of the keys."

A puzzled expression crossed the house manager's face. "Keys?"

"*Las llaves?*" Chanel translated, trying to be helpful.

Señora Reynosa nodded her understanding. "There are no locks at Villa Soler."

When the señora was gone, the Cheetahs gathered in the living room. Galleria gestured to their surroundings. "All this, and we get to sing, too? Say it loud now . . . it's—"

"Cheetah-licious!" everyone cried . . . except Chanel.

Galleria grabbed her friend's arm. "Enough pouting from you."

But Chanel pulled away and stubbornly shook her head. "Did you check her out?" She launched into a cruel imitation of Señora Reynosa. "'There are no locks at Villa Soler!' Everything is perfect here in Luc Land, huh? Why doesn't he just sell tickets?"

"I do host an enormous Christmas charity ball, but that's the closest I come," a strong, masculine voice informed her.

A tall, strikingly handsome man stood in the doorway. His jaw was firm and his hair black, with hints of silver at the temples. He wore a white linen suit without a tie. The man locked eyes with Chanel in an unwavering gaze, but his smile was warm.

"*Hola*, Chanel," he said sincerely.

Chanel was cool in her reply. "Thank you for having us, Luc," she said formally, refusing to speak Spanish with him.

The girls shook hands with Luc.

"Dorinda, Aquanette, Galleria, so good to see you again," Luc said warmly.

Dó giggled. "Everything is prettier here," she told him. "Even our names."

"On the contrary," Luc said, taking her hand, "Spain is more beautiful now that the Cheetah Girls have arrived."

All the girls swooned, except Chanel. She rolled her eyes.

"So make yourselves at home. I will join you in the morning. *Buenas noches*, Señoritas Cheetahs," Luc said. Then he departed.

"See what I'm talking about?" Chanel snapped after he'd gone. "'*Make yourselves at home! Get some sleep!*' He's so . . . *controlling*!"

Chanel made a face. But Aqua ignored it. "He's perfect! If your mom doesn't marry Luc," she threatened in her cowgirl twang, "give me a few years and I will. Good night!"

"We do need some sleep," Galleria said. "Big day. We're meeting the festival director tomorrow." She turned toward Chanel and gave her a hug. "Everything's going to be all right."

But Chanel wasn't so sure.

The next morning, the Cheetahs sat down on the carriage house terrace for breakfast. Dorothea and Juanita were already sipping coffee when the girls joined them around the beautifully set table.

As the girls ate and talked, they soaked up the atmosphere. The day was gorgeous. The sun was warm, but the breeze from the distant Mediterranean felt refreshingly cool.

"You girls think you can get around well enough on your own?" Dorothea asked. She, Juanita, and Luc were planning to spend the day in Sitges, a beach town south of Barcelona.

"Don't worry, Auntie Dorothea," Aqua replied, flashing her guidebook. "I've got it covered."

"And when she doesn't know what she's talking about, I'm here to translate," Chanel noted.

Galleria finished her freshly squeezed orange juice. "Today, we're going to drop by the festival headquarters and pick up our information packet."

Just then, Luc appeared and kissed Juanita. Luc attempted to hug Chanel, but she went limp, so he quickly backed away.

Chanel leaped to her feet.

"Well, then, we're off!" she loudly announced.

The girls were still finishing their last bites of breakfast, but they got the hint and gathered their things.

He smiled at the girls. "Just so you know, I

asked one of my associates, the Count de Tovar, to make himself available to you throughout your stay. You'll meet him later today."

Chanel's expression turned angry. Through clenched teeth, she began to say: "We don't need—" But Juanita stopped her daughter short with a hidden tug to the back of her hair.

"We don't need you *to go to any trouble*, Luc," Juanita quickly finished. "But they're happy to meet any friends and counts of yours."

"It's no trouble at all," Luc insisted.

Chanel didn't say another word. Furious that Luc would arrange for some stuffy aristocrat to spy on them, she herded her friends out of the room.

"Like we need some old count to babysit us!" she ranted when they were alone.

The Cheetah Girls found their own way to the Palau de la Musica headquarters. The building was on the northern end of Las Ramblas near Placa Catalunya.

Once inside, a female receptionist examined their papers. "So, the Cheetah Girls from New York."

"Yes." Galleria smiled. "Have voices, will travel."

"And your manager?" the receptionist asked. "Dorothea Garibaldi?"

Chanel jumped in. "She's—"

Galleria slapped her hand over Chanel's mouth. "Completely supportive. We're really fortunate."

"Not so fortunate. She neglected to sign the consent form. You must have an adult sign. The festival director has made a special trip to meet you today, at great expense to his schedule. We have already made concessions for you. He will not come back for you again." The woman started to hand the forms back to Galleria.

"We can't let a little thing like ink keep us from . . . We'll just stop around the corner and give her a buzz. We'll see if we can't work this out," Galleria replied.

The Cheetahs huddled in a corner.

"Our moms are at the beach," Chanel moaned. "They couldn't get here in time even if they left now!

"What are we going to do?" asked Dorinda.

"Bribe her," Aqua suggested. "That's how we do it back home."

"With what?" Dorinda snapped. "Our metro passes?"

"Chill, Cheetahs!" Galleria commanded. "Let our *manager* handle this." She whipped out her cell phone and dialed the festival number.

"Yes, hello. Is this the New Voices competition?" Galleria purred, imitating her mother's imperious voice. "This is Dorothea Garibaldi. My clients, the Cheetah Girls, have told me about this little mix-up. Here's the problem. I'm visiting my client, Djark, in Iceland. I'm absolutely dying to get to Barcelona to sign all the papers, but the airport is, of all things, iced in—"

The receptionist tried to interrupt, but Galleria plowed ahead. "So here's my fix. Fax the form to my girl in New York. She'll fax it to me. I'll sign and fax it back. A lot of work, I know darling, but I do this all the time."

"I wish I could accommodate you, Mrs. Garibaldi," the receptionist replied, "but there's one problem."

"I'll fix it," Galleria replied. "That's what I do."

"Iceland is actually quite warm this time of year. . . ."

Unfortunately, the receptionist's last reply hadn't come through the phone. It came from right behind the huddled Cheetahs.

The girls turned to find the woman frowning at them. *Busted!*

The girls' hearts sunk. Galleria wasn't ready to give up though. "We've worked so hard to get here! Can't we just talk to the director? My mom will sign the paperwork later. She's out at the beach."

"With my mom and her boyfriend, Señor Luc Bruyere," added Chanel.

"Señor Bruyere? You're acquainted with Luc Bruyere?" the receptionist asked.

"That's right," said Galleria, stepping forward. "We're staying at Villa Soler. He's our host."

The receptionist reached out for the paperwork. "I'll confirm this with Señor Bruyere. He's been a patron of the festival for years." Then, she pointed the way upstairs, where the director was waiting for them.

6

The theater was ten times the size of Manhattan Magnet's auditorium! (Can you say "intimidating"?!) And the unsmiling festival director was a tough audience. But the Cheetahs knew it was time to step up.

They sung their hearts out, then waited for the word. The festival director stood, straightened his tie, and told them they were officially entered in the New Voices competition!

Later that day, the Cheetah Girls were back at Luc's villa, relaxing and celebrating. They'd spent the afternoon sightseeing, and they were exhausted! With cold drinks in hand, Aqua, Dorinda, and Chanel dropped onto the outdoor furniture in the mansion's courtyard, where they had a magnificent view of the orchards and vineyards.

Aqua's satisfied sigh broke the silence. "Is it me, or is everything so peaceful?"

Dorinda sipped her fruity drink and stretched like a contented cat in her lounge chair. Like Aqua and Chanel, she felt limp as a noodle from their audition and hours of sightseeing. "I think I'm in a trance," she declared.

Chanel nodded. "This does beat a hot New York rooftop."

Suddenly, Galleria appeared and the mood changed. Still bubbling with energy, she handed each Cheetah a sheet of paper.

"I've made up our rehearsal schedule," Galleria explained.

"Galleria!" Chanel groaned, tossing the paper aside. "We just started to relax!"

Galleria shrugged. "I know. Bad idea. Vacation is over."

Aqua scanned the paper and made a face. "When are we going to see the Sagrada Familia?"

Galleria placed her hands on her hips. "This is the big time, Cheetahs. We have to step up our game. And we have no idea who our competition is."

"There's only one way to find out," a stranger's voice interrupted. "Ask the Dancing Cat."

The Cheetahs turned their heads to find a major-league hottie who had joined them in the courtyard. Tall and muscular, the twenty-year-old was deeply tanned, and had flashing dark eyes and a scorching smile. His rags were casual but elegant, designer from head to toe. But the Cheetahs hardly noticed the clothes. They were too busy buggin' over the boy's sudden appearance.

"Even as I said that, it sounded silly," the hot guy said with a laugh. "Señor Luc asked me to introduce myself. I'm Joaquin."

Aqua was the first Cheetah to regain her ability to speak. "You're the 'associate'?" she stammered.

"That's a fancy name for 'summer intern,' but I'll take it." Joaquin grinned again, and once more interfered with the Cheetahs' ability to form a coherent sentence. "Let's see—"

He walked over to Chuchie and offered his hand. "Chanel, right?"

Chanel speechlessly nodded.

Next, he faced Aqua. "Dorinda?" he asked, shaking her hand. Aqua was too awestruck to correct him.

"Aqua?" he said, taking Galleria's hand. Galleria stared dumbly.

Then he faced Dorinda. "And you must be Galleria," he said. Locking eyes with Dó, he *kissed* her hand!

"You got it all wrong, but nice try," Dó said, trying to keep her head. But her heart was pounding so fast and loud, she was sure everyone could hear it.

"Story of my life," Joaquin replied, still gazing into Dorinda's eyes. "It's a lovely hand, regardless."

"What's all this about a dancing cat," Dó asked, withdrawing her hand.

"Señor Luc tells me you're in the New Voices competition," Joaquin replied. "The Dancing Cat is a teen club. Everybody who's in the festival tries out their material there."

"Perfect!" Galleria cried. "We can peep who we're up against."

"Tomorrow night is open mic. I'll sign you up," offered Joaquin.

Suddenly, Luc appeared. "Good!" he exclaimed. "You've met Joaquin. He can show you around better than an old man like me."

"I've already bungled their names, Señor Luc," Joaquin replied. "It's downhill from here."

Chanel met Luc's eyes. "Luc, you said you were sending some stuffy old count to watch over us."

Luc laughed. "Old, no. Stuffy, rarely. But he is a count."

"Don't hold it against me," Joaquin protested.

"My brilliant godson. But the only way he's going to make it to Wall Street is if he spends less time on the dance floor," Luc noted.

Dorinda blinked in surprise. "You're a dancer?"

"A cutthroat competitor," Luc warned.

Aqua shook her head. "Dancing Cat? Dancing count? I'm dizzy."

Luc smiled. "Barcelona has that effect. I'll leave all you artists to your work. Dinner at ten, ladies."

As their host headed out the door, Galleria noticed that Dó and Joaquin were definitely checking each other out. Always thinking (a Cheetah trademark!), Galleria sidled up to the young count.

"Dorinda is our choreographer," she said.

"Maybe we can dance together while you're here this summer," Joaquin replied with a dramatic bow. He offered Dorinda his business card, looking deeply into her eyes. "My studio address. You are welcome to stop by tomorrow and meet some of the dancers."

The other Cheetahs answered for Dorinda. "She'll be there."

The next day, Dorothea, Galleria, and Aqua decided to do some window shopping.

The girls dressed for the occasion Cheetah

style—chic and trendy, with their favorite bling-bling and jungle-cat prints.

The weather was beautiful. It was a perfect day to take a stroll through the winding streets of the Barri Gòtic, Barcelona's gothic quarter. Dating back to the thirteenth century, this part of the city had a graceful, old-school European atmosphere.

Rounding a corner, the group came upon a store window filled with clothes that were just to their taste. As they headed inside to get a closer look at the fabulous merchandise, a well-dressed man stopped Dorothea.

"Dorothea?" asked the distinguished gentleman. "Dorothea Boucree?"

Dorothea nodded, startled. "Yes?" No one had called her by her maiden name in years!

"It's me," said the man with a smile, "Randolph Hunter."

"Oh, my gosh, Randolph," said Dorothea, surprised to see one of her closest friends from her modeling days. "This is unbelievable."

"And Francobollo? Is he here?" Randolph inquired.

"No, I'm here with my daughter and my best friend," Dorothea said, gesturing toward the group. "Franco's on a buying trip."

After a few more minutes of catching up, Randolph invited them inside. It turned out that he owned the store they liked so much— and it was filled with clothing designed by he and his wife, Aramet!

While Dorothea chatted with Randolph and Aramet, Galleria pulled Aqua aside. The Cheetah Girls had a lot of work to do before the New Voices competition, and time was running out.

"Let's try to do some rehearsing," she said to Aqua.

But Aqua was more interested in shopping. She hoped Randolph and Aramet would give her a discount on a beautiful dress she'd been eyeing.

Galleria was disappointed. She was beginning to wonder how they'd ever get their act together with so many distractions pulling them in different directions.

7

While Chanel spent the afternoon with her mother and Luc, Dorinda followed her feet to Joaquin's dance studio.

Dó couldn't believe the size of the place. Sunlight poured through the windows, illuminating a gleaming hardwood floor the size of two tennis courts. Ballet rails and mirrors ran along one wall, with benches near the door.

Whoa, she thought, this is the real thing. In the center of the floor, couples swirled to the passionate sound of tango music. That's where Dorinda saw him again—Joaquin. He was really in his element. Coupled with a skillful partner, he had total command of the session. As the other dancers twirled by, executing difficult moves, he called out corrections.

Finally, the music ended and Joaquin spotted Dorinda. "Come on, dance with me."

"I just came to say 'hi', and besides, I didn't bring any shoes," said Dorinda. But before she knew it, Joaquin had borrowed some shoes and even a tango skirt for Dorinda to wear!

As they stepped onto the dance floor together, Joaquin gave her a wink. "*Okay*," he cried to the others. "I'm going to slow everything down for New York! They're always six hours behind."

"We'll see about that, Barcelona," said

Whether near or far, the Cheetah Girls live
by their credo: find fame (pronto!), sing like
it's your last supper, and hang tight with
your crew like Krazy Glue!

Galleria "Bubbles" Garibaldi founded the Cheetah Girls with her best friend, Chuchie, and writes all the growl-licious lyrics for their platinum-bound songs.

Dorinda Rogers is the Cheetah's choreographer and is always ready to try out the most tricked-out dance moves.

"Si, es la verdad. Yes, it's true!" coos Chanel "Chuchie" Simmons. "I'm a shop-happy señorita who wants to sing with *la mia amigas* for life— *pura vida!*"

"Yes, ma'am, I *am* the powerhouse voice of the group," declares sassy Aquanette Walker, thanks to her gospel roots homegrown in Houston, Texas.

Even though the New Voices competition was held in
Barcelona, Spain, the Cheetah Girls pounced on the
opportunity to flex their
"growl power" to the max.

Chanel loved shopping on Barcelona's Las Ramblas, a legendary street lined with cafés, galleries, and boutiques.

After meeting Dorothea's friend Randolph, a clothing designer, Aqua was excited to try her hand at sketching some designs of her own!

At the studio, Joaquin was impressed by how quickly Dorinda picked up the complicated tango moves.

When the Cheetahs sang Galleria's newest song, *"Amigas Cheetahs,"* the audience at the New Voices competition went wild.

The Cheetah Girls forever!

Dorinda, ready for the challenge.

Within minutes, Dó was relaxing into the music, letting her love of dance overcome her anxieties. Her natural talent was immense, and Joaquin was impressed at the speed she picked up every new move. The other dancers were impressed, too.

Dorinda learned several combination moves and then some more advanced steps. Even after hours on her feet, Dorinda felt as if she were dancing on clouds. With this boy, every move felt effortless.

As the day progressed, the shadows lengthened and the rest of the world melted away. Couples left the floor until there was only the music and Joaquin. Finally, he spun Dorinda one last time and dipped her. When he lifted her, they were face-to-face, close enough to kiss.

"That was fun, New York," Joaquin said. "You were great."

"No, you're great," Dorinda said. Then,

looking at a clock, she realized she was late. "I've got to go!"

He smiled down at her. "Not before you promise to come back and teach a hip-hop class," he said.

"Sure," Dó replied.

"There's a beach party tomorrow night. Say you'll come with me," Joaquin said insistently.

"I'm sure we'll be rehearsing," Dó said, as she took off the dance shoes and ducked behind a curtain to change out of the borrowed skirt and back into her own clothes.

"You have to take a break sometime. Bring all the Cheetahs," he said.

Dorinda slung her bag over her shoulder and headed for the door. "Maybe. Thanks again for the . . . tango," she said before dashing down the stairs to the street below.

That evening, the Cheetahs made their way through the crowds on Las Ramblas and entered the rockin' nightclub called the Dancing Cat.

Beneath flashing neon lights, fashion-forward young people sat at tables or stood laughing and talking in tight clusters. On the dance floor, couples moved to the bangin' beat of a live band.

Dorinda spotted Joaquin, who was sitting at a table with a few other guys. As the Cheetahs approached, they all stood, offering the girls their seats. "*Hola*, Cheetahs!" Joaquin said. He leaned in to give Dorinda a European-style, double-cheeked kiss. The other Cheetahs noticed the difference in treatment—all they got were polite smiles!

"Joaquin, this place is off the chain," Galleria cried, bobbing her head to the pounding beat.

"I see lots of the contestants here tonight," Joaquin said as the girls sat down.

"Good. Maybe we'll break them off a little girl power," Galleria purred. "Let them know growl power is in the house."

Just then, the music changed tempo. A hot young girl moved onto the stage. She had gorgeous hair, delicate features, long-lashed eyes, and her outfit was Euro chic.

"Who's that?" Chanel asked.

"That's Marisol, a homegrown favorite," answered Joaquin. "Barcelona's best chance to win the competition.

The girl stepped onto the stage and began to belt out a song. Her voice was polished, her act tight. Marisol easily sealed the deal with the cheering Dancing Cat crowd—they gave her much love.

The Cheetahs applauded politely.

"So how about that growl power?" Joaquin asked.

Galleria glanced at her crew.

"I'm exhausted," said Dorinda.

"My jet lag's kicking in," Chanel agreed.

Aqua fanned herself. "It's really hot in here."

Galleria knew what was really up. Trying to show up a talented homegirl on her own turf wasn't on the top of their to-do list tonight. She turned to Joaquin. "We'll sing another night," she said.

Joaquin shrugged. "No problem, ladies. Thirsty?" They nodded, and he took off with his friends to get more sodas for the girls. While he was gone, a handsome young street performer took to the stage—someone the Cheetah Girls all recognized.

"We're going to slow things down a little at the Dancing Cat," Angel announced as he positioned his guitar.

"This guy is *everywhere*," Galleria said.

Angel began to sing a song in Spanish that was beautiful and sad and filled with longing.

"My mom used to sing this song to me all the time," Chanel whispered.

Chanel was so moved she began to sing along. Soon her voice was joined with Marisol's, who was sitting at the next table with an older woman.

Angel stopped singing, letting only his guitar accompany the beautiful duet of female voices—Chanel's and Marisol's.

Chanel motioned for the other Cheetahs to join in, and the sweet five-part harmony flowed over the room like melodic honey. When the song ended, the applause nearly took off the nightclub's roof.

"From New York: the Cheetah Girls!" cried Joaquin, who'd returned to the table with their soft drinks.

More cheers followed, and Marisol rose from her table to greet the girls. "The *Cheetah* Girls?" she said, a puzzled expression on her face.

The older woman from Marisol's table got up to join her. "Americans, is that right?" she asked. "Singing in the contest?"

"This is my mother, Lola Duran," Marisol said.

"You girls are so talented!" Lola cried. "Did you travel here alone?"

"No, our mothers are here," Galleria replied. Then she winked at Marisol. "My mother is our manager, too. I know one when I see one."

Lola laughed. "I'd love to meet your mother. Marisol, give Chanel and the girls our cell number. We should all get together. How's tomorrow?"

"Cool," said Galleria. "What's your big, long Spanish phone number?"

"Why don't I just give it to you," Lola said to Chanel. Chanel handed Lola her cell phone so she could program the number. "It's easier to speak in Spanish, you know. . . ."

Chanel nodded. "And here's my phone number," she said as she put her own number into Lola's phone.

"Perfect. May I give you a little insight? It's very hard to win the contest on your first try. We know, don't we, darling," Lola said quietly, taking her daughter's hand.

"That's right, Mom," Marisol replied uncomfortably. "This is my third try."

Then Lola grinned at the Cheetah Girls. "I'll open some doors for you if you like. Think of me as your Spanish mama!"

8

The next morning, Galleria told her mother about Lola's offer to help them. The two were walking through the Barcelona marketplace. Dó, Aqua, and Chanel were listening right behind them.

"Don't you think it's a little strange that this woman wants to help you girls?" Dorothea asked her daughter.

"Mom, this is Spain. People are warm and

generous. She wants to make Spain a great experience for us," Galleria said.

Dorinda caught up. "Even Joaquin says everybody knows her. She's kind of a big deal around here."

Aqua jabbed Dó playfully. "Is *that* what Joaquin said?"

Galleria tried to convince her mom that everything would be okay. "She insisted on meeting you. Now what does that tell you?"

Dorothea raised an eyebrow. "She's smart."

Not far away, Marisol listened as her mother laid out the plan.

"Stay with Chanel," commanded Lola. "Let her help you with your English, and make sure you teach her your contest number. And the dance steps."

Marisol sighed. "What are you trying to do, Mom? Are you trying to break up the Cheetah Girls?"

Lola clutched her daughter's arm. "You heard it last night. When you and Chanel sing together, it's magic. You two are perfect partners."

Marisol was hurt. "I don't want to do this. It's wrong. I worked so hard this year to be ready. Why won't you believe in me?"

"Listen to me, Marisol. You've lost twice already. If we lose again, it's over," Lola hissed. "You and Chanel together are magic. You heard the crowd. Together, you can go to the top. Isn't this our dream?"

But before Marisol could reply, Dorothea and the Cheetah Girls appeared right in front of them.

"*Hola*, Lola! Hey, Marisol!" exclaimed Chanel.

"*Hola*, Cheetahs!" said Marisol.

Suddenly, Lola's scowl turned into a beaming smile. "Welcome to Spain!" she said, sizing up Dorothea. "Your girls are magnificent!"

Dorothea nodded coolly. "We think we'll keep them."

The Cheetahs and Marisol exchanged uneasy glances. It was obvious Dorothea didn't like Lola. But the girls liked each other just fine. Gritting their teeth, they wondered why the adults couldn't just get out of the way!

Late that afternoon, the Cheetahs decided to forget their worries by checking out Joaquin's beach party. Hundreds of kids had assembled at the water's edge. Music pumped and bodies danced, bare feet splashing in the foaming surf.

Galleria, Chanel, Aqua, and Dorinda relaxed on lounge chairs in the warm, white sand, looking growl-licious in Cheetah-spotted sunglasses, swimsuits, and wrap skirts.

Joaquin was in line, waiting to order some food, but all the girls noticed that he was watching Dorinda the whole time.

Galleria sighed. "So, how do you say 'boyfriend' in Spanish?"

"*Novio*!" Aqua and Chanel said in unison.

Chanel poked Aqua. "That one you say perfectly," she teased.

"That was the first Spanish word I learned." Aqua laughed. "Okay, the first word was 'nachos'. But 'boyfriend' was right up there."

"He's not my boyfriend," Dorinda said firmly. "He's teaching me tango. I'm teaching him some hip-hop. I'm getting some fresh ideas that we might be able to incorporate into the show."

Galleria immediately started trippin'. She liked this party fine, but she *lived* for the Cheetah Girls. "Show us, come on!" She jumped out of her chair. "Everybody's dancing—we could squeeze in some rehearsal."

Aqua and Chanel exchanged unhappy glances and sighed. Grudgingly, they hauled their bodies up from their comfortable seats.

Dorinda led them to an empty space on the sand. The Cheetahs were fast learners. Soon all four were performing a thrillin' hip-hop–style tango.

Before the song ended, Joaquin appeared with a plate of delicious-looking food. "No, no!" he cried. "No work today. This is a party. Marco made some tapas." Then he gestured toward Marco, who was giving the girls a friendly wave. "There's plenty more on the patio."

"Tapas with Marco. I like that in English *or* Spanish!" Aqua said before heading off to introduce herself.

Joaquin forgot all about the food he'd just brought, and spun Dorinda onto the sand. A slow song flowed over the crowd, and he pulled her close.

Galleria pulled Chanel aside. "So Chuchie, about rehearsal."

Just then, Marisol came walking up to the girls. "Chanel! I've been looking for you everywhere. I want to introduce you to some friends."

Chanel started to follow Marisol, but Galleria stopped her. "Chuchie, one hour, okay? We've got to have a game plan."

But after an hour had passed, there was still no sign of Chanel. Frustrated, Galleria plopped into a lounge chair. We haven't rehearsed in days, she thought. But we better get it together soon, or we might as well get gone!

"So much for growl power," she muttered.

The hours flew by. As afternoon turned into evening, the kids lit a huge bonfire, sending orange flames into a purple sky.

Away from the throbbing music, Dorinda and Joaquin sat on a blanket among the sand dunes, watching the foamy waves wash ashore.

"So I guess I have to ask," said Dó. "How do you become a count?"

Joaquin smiled. "I guess my great-great-grandfather was friends with the right people. Or *not* friends with the wrong people. I forget which."

Dó laughed. "Being royal sounds like high school."

Joaquin nodded. "You're starting to get the picture. What about you? Does your family support your dreams?"

Dó shifted uneasily. She wasn't ashamed of being a foster child. But she wondered whether an aristocrat would really accept someone with her background. "Let's talk about it another time," she said.

Joaquin grinned. "Good. That means there'll be another time."

Meanwhile, on the other side of the beach, Galleria stood alone, gazing at the rising moon.

"Galleria!" a familiar voice called.

Galleria turned to see her gypsy friend walking toward her. "Angel! Hey."

"Why did you leave the party?" he asked.

"It looks like fun. And where are your friends, *sus amigas* Cheetahs?"

Galleria sighed. "My *amigas* Cheetahs? They're starting to get on my nerves."

"Ah, Cheetahs, but maybe not *amigas*," Angel said.

"No! We're friends for life," she assured him. "Don't try to understand it. It's a girl thing."

Angel pulled the guitar from his back and began to play. Galleria smiled and took out her tiny recorder. "Friends for life," she said quietly. "Thank you. Good night, Angel."

Angel gazed after Galleria as she walked away. "*Hasta pronto*, Galleria."

The next morning, Dorothea and Juanita were eating breakfast on the terrace.

"There's something about that Lola character that isn't quite right," Dorothea said. "But she's a little hard to read."

Juanita knew just what she was talking about. "You know who's hard to read? Luc. He brings me all the way to Spain, and no ring?"

"They promised me this would be a trouble-free trip. My heart tells me to keep an eye on this woman, though. Mama Cheetah doesn't play when it comes to her cubs," Dorothea said. "More tea?"

"Love some," Juanita responded.

Inside, the Cheetah Girls were resisting Galleria's push to rehearse. Tired and distracted, they dragged themselves to the piano in the guesthouse common room. But their warm-up sounded anything but tight.

Galleria lifted her fingers from the piano keys and frowned at her friends. "Okay, let's take it again."

Aqua groaned. "Let's take a nap again. The party was bananas! And I can't bounce back like I could when I was twelve."

Galleria opened one of her notebooks and propped it up on the piano. "We've only been rehearsing for half an hour. I want to play you this song I've been work-ing on."

But before she could start, Chanel said, "Hey, I wanted to tell you guys. Lola says it might be a good idea for us to learn a Spanish song."

"But we don't speak Spanish," Galleria pointed out.

Just then, the phone rang in the other room. "Señorita Dorinda? *Telephono*," Señora Reynosa called.

Dorinda picked up the extension with a smile on her face. As she started to talk qui-etly, the Cheetahs rolled their eyes. They knew it had to be Joaquin.

"Chanel, did you forget we're going to lunch today with Luc's family?" asked Juanita, coming in off the terrace with Dorothea.

Before Galleria knew it, Chuchie was being dragged off, and Dorothea was on her way out for the day, too. "I'm going to

Aramet's fashion studio for the day. Have a good rehearsal."

"Later, Mom," Galleria replied. She turned to Aqua. "We have four days until the competition. It's ridiculous to learn a new song in Spanish."

"I think . . . Auntie Dorothea! Wait up!" said Aqua, who'd suddenly decided that she'd rather go shopping than talk about the competition.

Snap, Galleria thought, seeing her mother and Aqua head out the door. *I'm losing everyone!*

The last Cheetah left was Dorinda. But when she ended her call, she was as good as gone, too.

"Joaquin wants me to teach a hip-hop class at noon!" she cried excitedly.

"Go, go, go," Galleria said, hiding her disappointment. "When in Spain . . ."

As she watched the last other Cheetah Girl head out the door, Galleria frowned and murmured, "*Amigas* Cheetahs, friends for life."

The afternoon flew by for all the Cheetahs. At Joaquin's studio, Dorinda taught a group of Barcelona's best dancers the hottest hip-hop steps off the New York streets.

Chanel was on her best behavior meeting Luc's family. They were warm, loving, and a lot more fun than she ever dreamed.

Galleria spent the afternoon at the piano, working on the song and scribbling lyrics into her notebook.

Finally, Aqua accompanied Dorothea to Aramet and Randolph's fashion house, where she had an *amazing* time. One minute she was watching Aramet work on a ball gown, and the next—with Dorothea's encourage-ment—she was helping the woman redesign it!

Dorothea was thrilled watching Aqua discover her hidden talent. As Aramet worked with the girl, Randolph sidled up to Dorothea. "Takes me back to when you were in design school. That joy and passion," he whispered.

Dorothea smiled. "A little bit . . . Okay, a *lot*."

"It's never too late," said Randolph.

But Dorothea waved the thought aside. "I was just helping her. She's got a good eye."

"Why did you let it go, Dorothea?" Randolph asked.

"I didn't let it go," she replied. "The deadlines, the travel—getting to the top would have meant dragging my daughter all over the world. Or never getting to tuck her in at night. I didn't want to do both things if I had to do them both poorly."

"And now that she's all grown up, what's next?" he pressed.

Dorothea didn't have an answer for that.

The next morning, Galleria burst into the common room bubbling with energy.

"Cheetahs," she cried, "I've written the best song in my life and I can't wait to show it to you. We ready to get down?"

No one replied. The guesthouse was empty. She found Aqua and Dó on the terrace. Aqua was sketching a dress design. Dó was on the phone.

"Good, you guys are up and moving. I want you to hear something!" Galleria said excitedly.

"Cool. And wait till you see what your mom and I have dreamed up for you! It's for the festival!" said Aqua.

Dorothea walked in. "Hey, sleepyhead," she said, "how did you like the sketches?"

Galleria glanced at the designs and put them aside. "These outfits are amazing, Mom, but we have to focus on song charts before costume sketches."

Dorothea agreed. "And you have to have breakfast before any of it."

As Galleria headed toward the kitchen, she heard Dorinda say, "Great. I'll leave right now." She was still on the phone.

"Where are you going?" Galleria asked. "We have rehearsal."

"Hold on." Dó covered the phone. "He invited me to lunch," she explained.

Galleria was losing patience. "Aqua's gone. Now we've lost Dó."

Just then, Galleria heard Chanel laughing out on the terrace. "Who's out there with Chanel?" Galleria wondered aloud. Walking outside, she saw Chanel and Marisol singing a Spanish pop song in harmony.

Galleria folded her arms. "Well, at least somebody's rehearsing something."

"This is one of Marisol's songs," Chanel explained. "She's teaching me the words. We're just fooling around."

Galleria rolled her eyes. "Marisol, look, I

don't mean to sound controlling, but we really have to rehearse. You should really go."

"I was invited here, Galleria," Marisol said defensively. "I didn't just drop by."

Chuchie was in no mood to be pushed around. Yesterday, she'd spent a ton of time with Luc's family. But in the end, it hadn't mattered. Yet again, Luc had failed to pop the question. And her mom's disappointment was hard to take. "Since when do you tell me when my friends can hang with me and when they can't? You need to chill, Galleria, and give me my space," she said.

"Your space? We're in this space because of you!" Galleria pulled Chanel aside. "What's going on here? Are you choosing her over the Cheetah Girls? What happened to our promise? I'm doing this for you, Chanel."

But Chanel didn't believe her. "I question that. Come on, Marisol."

❖ ❖ ❖ ❖ ❖ ❖ ❖ ❖ ❖ ❖ ❖ ❖ ❖ ❖ ❖ ❖ ❖ ❖

Devastated, Galleria tried to pull herself together. She went back into the villa, where she found Aqua looking at the sketches and Dorinda walking out the door. "See you guys later," she said.

"What time is later?" Galleria shouted. "Are we going to rehearse or not? Are we going to be in the competition or not?"

"It's not like we're not working on the dances," Dorinda pointed out. "Relax."

"But how can you choreograph a number when we haven't even picked out a song?" asked Galleria.

"Everybody come to the dance studio around three. We'll get started then. It'll all be fine," said Dorinda, closing the door behind her.

"Nobody's taking this seriously but me," Galleria said.

Dorothea placed her hands on her hips. "Galleria, calm down. This whole experience isn't about winning. The universe sent you here, remember? Now let the universe be your guide. You can't control everything."

No one's listening to me anymore, Galleria thought. Before we came here, we were four girls with one dream, she realized. Now I have to face reality. My best friends have other dreams—and I'm just standing in their way.

10

Dorinda thought Joaquin looked extra-yummy today, still dressed for his internship in a designer suit and silk tie. Some of his friends from work were at the studio with him, trying to convince him to join them for lunch.

The people were very different from his easygoing dance-studio friends. These young men and women were all formally dressed in tailored suits and designer dresses. One member of the group, a tall, leggy blond, laughed at Joaquin's joke. She pushed him flirtatiously.

Finally, Joaquin spied Dorinda. She waved at him, and he waved back but then turned back to his group once again. Then, to Dorinda's dismay, a few of them snuck a look at her. What were they saying? She was suddenly self-conscious and uncomfortable.

At last, Joaquin sent off his friends. As they left the studio, the leggy blond raised an eyebrow at Dorinda.

"Hey there, ready for lunch?" Joaquin asked, walking up to her.

"I could have dressed up if I'd known," Dó said.

Joaquin's brow wrinkled. "What do you mean? Barcelona's casual. We can eat anywhere."

"Why did you send your friends off?" Dó snapped.

Joaquin blinked. "I didn't send them off, I—"

"Yes you did, and you didn't introduce me," Dorinda cried, angry and hurt. "I guess I'm fine to hang out with your dance pals, but when the suits come out, we're just from two different worlds."

"Different?" said Joaquin. "I don't think I've ever met anybody more like me in my life."

Dó just shook her head. "We are not alike. You can trace your family back for centuries. I have no idea who my real family is. Dancing for you is a hobby. Dancing, for me, is my whole life. Maybe I don't know where I come from, but I know who I am and where I'm going. And it's not here."

"I didn't know any of this," Joaquin said, confused as he watched Dorinda turn and walk out the studio door.

*L*ater that evening, Dorothea and Galleria were alone on the terrace. Dorothea pulled out a sketch pad and showed a drawing of a wedding dress to her daughter.

"What do you think?" she asked.

"It's amazing, Mom," said Galleria. "Has *Madrina* seen it?" Galleria had heard Chanel calling Dorothea *Madrina*. Galleria thought the word had a nice ring to it and sometimes called Juanita *Madrina*, even though Juanita was Galleria's aunt—not her godmother.

"No, not yet. But Aramet and Randolph love it and want to do a sample for the spring," Dorothea replied, clearly thrilled by the idea of designing clothes again.

"I haven't seen you so happy in a long time, Mom," Galleria said quietly.

"I figured something out on this trip," her mother responded.

"What, Mom?" asked Galleria.

"I gave up my dream of being a couture

designer because I was scared," Dorothea admitted. "I had the talent, but I wanted a guarantee. I was too afraid to jump before I knew where I was going to land. Then you were born, and raising you right became the most important thing of all."

"You could have done both, Mom," said Galleria.

"I made the right choice," her mother said warmly.

"I'm scared, too, Mom," Galleria said finally. "Just like you. That's why I'm going home."

Dorothea couldn't believe what she was hearing. "What?"

"Chanel's found a new friend in Marisol. She lives here. They speak the same language. They connect. I think she's really helping her through the situation," Galleria said, knowing how much Chanel was struggling with her mother's relationship with Luc. "I love Chanel, but I need to back off. If I don't, I may lose her as a friend, which is more important to me than win-ning this competition. I want her to be happy."

Dorothea was starting to understand. "I know how you feel, but . . ."

"I can't stay here being mad at everybody because they want to have fun. They want to be girls more than Cheetah Girls right now. And that's okay. It's time for me to leave."

"Okay, honey. We'll leave tomorrow," Dorothea said, putting a hand on her daughter's shoulder.

"Your dreams are here," Galleria said, picking up her mother's sketch. "And it's time for you to go after them. Plus you've got to stay here. Tia Juanita needs you. I talked to Daddy. He's got a layover in Paris, so I'm taking the train tomorrow and meet-ing him. We'll fly home together. We'll see what happens with the Cheetah Girls later. I don't know where I'm going to land, Mom, but I know I have to jump."

"I raised a fearless girl," Dorothea said, reaching out to hug her daughter. "I love you."

Later that night, when Aqua, Dó, and Chanel finally returned to the villa, Juanita and Dorothea broke the bad news.

"What do you mean, Galleria is leaving?!" Chanel cried. "Is this true?"

"She thinks her Spain experience is over, and she's okay with it," answered Dorothea.

"She's *that* mad at me? Let me talk to her," Chanel begged.

But Dorothea stood her ground. "She's made her decision. She's getting some sleep now."

Aqua dropped into a chair. "I guess we've been distracted."

Dorinda was angry at herself. "I wasted so much time *dancing around*," she said bitterly. "I wasn't there for her."

"She thinks I dumped her for Marisol," Chanel said softly.

"You did," Aqua pointed out.

"And you know that *how*, Miss Fashion Design Diva?" Chanel snapped.

Dorothea stepped between them. "Galleria has made her own decision. She's doing what she thinks is best."

"But I really want to talk to her—" Chanel started.

Juanita looked at her daughter. "Sometimes people just need their space, even Cheetahs. Let her get some sleep. Talk with her in the morning."

The next morning, Chanel knocked on Galleria's door. Yawning and still wearing their pajamas, Aqua and Dorinda joined her. They knocked again, but there was no reply. Finally, Chanel opened the door.

Galleria was already gone.

The room was empty except for some sheet music on the bed. Chanel picked it up. "*'Amigas* Cheetahs,'" she read and began to sing the words.

The other Cheetahs gathered around, taking in the sound of Galleria's masterpiece. Then they ran to the villa's chauffeur, who brought around the limo. As they drove to the train station, Chanel's cell rang.

"Marisol!" she answered. "I can't talk. We have a big problem. Galleria's leaving Barcelona. She's gone! I'll call you back."

Meanwhile, at the Barcelona train station, Galleria walked calmly toward her train, tickets in hand. She'd been here only an hour, but already she had that dazed look most travelers get from waiting around in endless lines.

Suddenly she stopped walking. Blinking, she looked around. Did she just hear the lyrics of her song? Or was she daydreaming?

Galleria whirled and saw Dorinda, Aqua, and Chanel, still wearing their pajamas, singing her song!

Chanel stepped forward as the song ended. "This was written for four-part harmony," she told Galleria. "We can't do it without you, girl. It's the best song you've ever written. Forgive me?"

Galleria ran to the girls. They hugged and jumped and squealed and cried. "It was my fault. . . . No, my fault . . . I'm sorry. . . ."

"It's okay, Cheetahs," Galleria finally said, wiping away her tears. "Let's go!"

11

The Cheetahs immediately returned to the villa and started planning their strategy for the New Voices competition.

"We're ready to focus and work," Dorinda said. "There's still time."

"Are you guys sure?" asked Galleria.

"No doubt," replied Aqua with a smile. "We've already made a million memories here, but I don't want to go home wondering what we could have done if we'd pulled it all together."

"We're all different, but we want the same thing," said Dorinda, nodding. "We want to be the best we can be. If we want it, we've got to work for it."

The Cheetahs put their hands together, and yelled, "Cheetah!" They were back on the prowl.

Just then, Chanel's cell rang. Chanel placed the phone in the center of the table and set it to speaker mode.

It was Lola. "*Chanel, amor. Digame—*"

Chanel stopped her. "Lola, I put you on speaker."

"I'm so sorry about what happened with Galleria," said Lola, "but—"

"No, Lola. I'm here!" Galleria said loudly. "That was just a little misunderstanding. I just want to let you know, the Cheetahs are ready to be fierce."

"So glad you're back," Lola replied. Her

tone was strained. "Because I'm booking a warm-up gig at the Dancing Cat on Wednesday night. We can talk about music choices later."

"Lola, Cheetahs pick their own music. Galleria's written her best song ever. We're singing it for the competition, and we've got plenty of material for a warm-up gig," Chanel said proudly.

"All right then, girls. Ciao for now!" Lola replied as she hung up the phone. She shot Marisol a dissatisfied look. "They're back together."

Marisol shrugged. "What did you want me to do? Put Galleria on the train myself?"

The next morning, Juanita and Dorothea were eating breakfast on the terrace. Chanel was about to join them, but stopped when she saw that her mother was clearly upset about something.

"He's crazy about you, honey. It's obvious," said Dorothea.

"His family welcomed us, and we have a great time together. Every day we have more in common and I love him more and more." Juanita frowned. "But I can't force things when they aren't meant to happen."

Still secretly listening, Chanel knew what she had to do. She went looking for Luc and found him in his private office. The door was open, but she knocked anyway. Luc saw her and stood up from his desk.

"Chanel, come in. Sit down," he said.

"I don't need to sit down, Luc," Chanel began. "I just want to say I'm sorry . . . about me and you and my mom and how I'm standing in the way like a spoiled brat. I'm sorry I didn't trust you."

"I plan to have a life with your mother," said Luc. "I want you to be part of that."

Chanel met his gaze. "I would be proud to be part of your family."

Later that morning, the Cheetahs, their moms, and Señor and Señora Reynosa all stood in a doorway, looking outside. They watched as Luc approached Juanita, who was sitting near the villa's outdoor fountain. Juanita turned and smiled. Then suddenly, Luc was down on his knees, a huge diamond ring resting in the palm of his hand. The jewel flashed in the sunlight, a brilliant promise.

"Yes!" Juanita cried, then stepped into Luc's waiting arms.

The happy couple was soon joined by the group, who cheered their wonderful news. Finally, my mom can be happy, thought Chanel.

Later that day, Dorinda was stretching on the dance studio's rooftop balcony. She was waiting for the other Cheetahs to start their dance rehearsal.

"Marco told me you were up here," Joaquin said, approaching her. "You haven't taken my calls for days,"

"Thank you for letting us use your dance space for our rehearsal," Dorinda said in a frosty tone.

"It's not my dance space. Luc owns this building, and I help with the rent by giving lessons and working in his office," Joaquin replied.

Dorinda took a step back. "What?"

"I didn't introduce you to those kids the other day because I couldn't afford to take you where they were going for lunch," Joaquin said, looking away.

"But you're . . ." Dó said.

"Yes, I'm a royal. And broke," Joaquin said, facing her. "Any money our family had was gone long ago. Knowing who your ancestors are isn't all it's cracked up to be."

Dorinda shook her head. She'd been so wrong about him.

Just then, the Cheetahs appeared in the doorway. "We're here and ready to tango," Galleria declared. But when they realized Dó and Joaquin were talking about something serious, the girls moved to the dance floor downstairs and began their stretches.

Joaquin put a hand on Dorinda's shoulder. "So you thought you came to Spain and found a prince, huh? The movie's over, New York. I'm just another dancer."

Dorinda felt a rush of guilt—and relief. "Joaquin, I'm so sorry for misreading, judging, and . . . I should know better."

"Don't apologize." He smiled. "Just dance with me."

"The girls are here. We have to rehearse," Dorinda said.

"No, I mean, I have a competition in New York this fall," he clarified. "Dance with me. Be my partner."

That night at the Dancing Cat, the Cheetah Girls played to a packed house. Tighter than tight, they strutted two old favorites, then delivered one new song for their brand-new European fans, saving "*Amigas* Cheetahs" for the festival itself.

After the show, the girls joined their family and friends. They talked for hours until Luc, Juanita, and Dorothea decided to call it a night.

When their parents were gone, the Cheetahs sat down with Joaquin, Lola, and Marisol. They wanted to thank Lola for arranging their appearance. As they sat down, the Dancing Cat's owner approached the table. He slipped an envelope into Galleria's hand.

"What's this?" Galleria asked.

"Your payment for tonight's work," the owner said.

Chanel turned to Lola. "Really?"

"You'll have expenses for the festival. Take it," Lola insisted.

Aqua couldn't believe their luck. "Thank you. Bedazzling isn't cheap over here. I had to dip into my after-tax discretionary emergency beautification funds."

"Okay, girls," Lola said, clapping her hands, "lights out early. Sound check tomorrow."

As the Cheetahs sang good night, Angel watched them from the shadows, where he sat tuning his guitar. When he saw the envelopes, a worried expression crossed his face.

The Cheetah Girls arrived at the New Voices competition early. Inside the vast, empty theater, soundmen were performing system checks. Stagehands were moving set pieces. Carrying their costumes in garment bags, the girls moved backstage to the dressing rooms.

Lola and Marisol were already there. The

Cheetahs hung up their costumes, and everyone exchanged a flurry of hugs.

"What can I say about these Aqua-Cheetah fashions?" Galleria whooped. "Can we just take a moment to celebrate? It's happening!"

But their celebration didn't last long.

"I need to speak to the Cheetah Girls," the festival director said as he walked up to the group.

Galleria gave him a big hug, too. "Come here, you fantastic man! You made this whole thing happen."

"You'll have to excuse her," Chanel explained. "She's in the middle of a dream come true."

The director frowned. "That makes my news even more upsetting. Apparently you girls performed last night at the Dancing Cat."

"That's right," Lola said. "I booked the show myself."

"And did you take any money for their performance?" the director asked.

"Me? No! I did not collect a centimo," Lola said indignantly. "They each took home one hundred euros for their hard work."

"Exactly," said the director. "Making them officially professionals. This is an amateur-only contest."

"What? What are you saying?" Galleria cried.

"The rules are very clear," the director replied. "There can be no performance by the Cheetah Girls on this stage tomorrow."

"They came all the way from New York for this!" Lola cried. "It was my mistake, don't punish them."

But the director was already leaving. "I'm very sorry," he said.

12

Galleria was near tears. "This can't be happening," she said, her voice a whisper.

"All this, for nothing!" Dorinda cried.

Chanel whipped out her cell phone. "I'm calling Luc. There's got to be something he can do."

"Wait a second," Lola said, putting a hand on Chanel's arm. "The Cheetah Girls can't perform. But Marisol can sing with you, and then you're not the Cheetah Girls anymore. It's dancing on the line, but at least you're in."

Galleria frowned. "Sing with us? She doesn't know our songs, and *hers* are in Spanish."

Marisol caught her mother's glance and jumped in with the line they'd already rehearsed. "*Chanel* knows a couple of my songs."

"But my girls don't," Chanel said firmly. "It's all of us or nothing."

Galleria grabbed her friend's arms. "We've come so far. The Cheetah Girls are going to be represented on that stage. That means you're going to sing, Chuchie."

"Marisol, are you sure?" Chanel asked.

Marisol glanced at the hard look in Lola's eyes. "Sure, I'll do it," the girl mumbled.

Lola forced a plastic smile and put an arm around her daughter. "The show must go on, right, girls?"

*B*ack at Luc's villa, Dorothea hit the roof when she heard the news. "I'm telling you, it's Lola. That woman! I knew it from the very beginning!" she raged. "You should have listened to me."

"She was only trying to help us," said Galleria.

Dorothea snorted. "There isn't an honest bone in that woman's body. Luc, is there anything you can do?"

"I can call a friend at the festival headquarters," he said hopefully.

Galleria knew they had to handle this problem on their own. "We got ourselves into this mess. Chanel is going to represent us. We would love it if you were all there tomorrow to support her."

"Don't worry, Cheetahs," Luc said. "When we're all back in New York, there will be more performances for you."

Chanel was confused. "We're going back to New York?"

Juanita smiled. "After the wedding, Luc's going to live with us."

"Really?" Chanel asked, her eyes bright.

"It's your senior year in high school," Luc said. "We wouldn't miss it for the world. And I'm not breaking up the Cheetah Girls!"

"There's one more thing we have to make right," announced Galleria.

The others looked at her with puzzled expressions. Galleria explained to her friends that before real Cheetah-prowlin' pride could kick in, they had to return the money they'd accepted from the Dancing Cat.

"You Americans can be so confusing," the club owner said a half hour later, when the girls handed back their envelopes.

"Let's just say it's the principle of the thing," Galleria told the owner as they walked away.

The start of the New Voices competition

was just minutes away. Backstage, the air was sizzling with excitement as performers warmed up their voices.

In their dressing room, the girls were getting into their Cheetah costumes with the help of Dorothea and Juanita. Chanel and Marisol practiced their first song, but their voices lacked spirit.

"Sounds good, girls," Lola said, striding in.

Finally seeing the woman, Dorothea confronted her. "This whole thing has hit quite a sour note, Lola," she said, anger in her voice.

Lola sighed. "I'm sorry they had to suffer on my account. But they're very flexible. You should be proud. They're going to make it, don't you worry."

Just then, the dressing room door opened. In walked Angel, followed by the festival director and Señor Antonio, the owner of the Dancing Cat!

"Angel," said Galleria, "what are you doing here?"

Angel smiled. "I'm here to play for the *Amigas* Cheetahs."

"I must correct a very grave error," the director announced, looking straight at Lola. "My nephew has informed me that you arranged for the Cheetah Girls to be paid after their performance at the Dancing Cat."

Galleria blinked. "Angel? You were there?"

The street musician smiled. "Yes, watching out for . . . how did you say it? The principle of the thing."

"So, the Cheetah Girls *will* perform?" Dorothea asked with hope.

Galleria crossed her fingers. "*All* of us? As the Cheetah Girls?"

The man nodded. "With my apologies, and my best wishes—in about half an hour."

"Wait a second," Lola snapped. "Those girls were disqualified. They took the money. They broke the rules."

"And they gave the money back," he

replied. "I don't need you to tell me the rules. I wrote them. The Cheetah Girls will perform."

The Cheetahs cheered and thanked the director and Angel.

Lola stopped Chanel and spoke to her in Spanish. "I could have taken Marisol and you to the top," she hissed.

Chanel snapped her fingers. "I'm already *at* the top. With my girls. And we're going to win—our way."

Lola looked down her nose at the Cheetahs. "Marisol will still perform," she said with a sneer. "And then we'll see, won't we?"

At that, Marisol ran from the dressing room, head down. Lola took off after her daughter. For a moment, there was silence in the room. But Dorothea soon broke it.

"Cheetahs! It's showtime!" she cried.

Forty-five minutes later, the Cheetah Girls were waiting backstage to make their entrance. The cheers from the packed auditorium swelled as another act took a final bow and exited the stage.

When the applause faded, the announcer's voice boomed through the vast theater. "And now, Barcelona's own—Marisol!"

Cheers and applause greeted the girl's name. But the enthusiastic response soon faded in confusion when the stage remained deserted.

"Will Marisol please take the stage?" the announcer asked. "Last call for Marisol!"

But Marisol refused to perform. As her mother searched backstage for her, Marisol slipped into the audience. At the back of the auditorium, she sat down with a soda, ready to enjoy the show—happier than she'd been in a very long time.

Finally, the judges in the front row crumpled Marisol's score sheet and signaled the announcer to move on to the next act.

"The final competitors in the Barcelona

New Voices competition are from New York City and Houston, Texas," the announcer's voice boomed.

Backstage, Galleria led a Cheetah chant.

"The Cheetah Girls!" the announcer cried.

A pool of light appeared onstage. Angel was in the center of it, guitar ready. The Cheetahs emerged from the wings, and Galleria took the microphone.

"This song is dedicated to Barcelona, where I found Angels around every corner. *Gracias*, Barcelona," Galleria said. The audience applauded warmly. "Thank you for teaching me that everyone's path is not the same. But when you find friends who will take the journey with you," Galleria continued, "they're your real *Amigas* Cheetahs!"

Galleria stepped back to join the others. Chanel stepped out of the shadows next, to begin a solo performance accompanied only by Angel's sweet guitar. But as the rhythm kicked in, the Cheetahs pounced—fiercer than they've ever been!

Dorinda led the Cheetahs into a tasty tango-style hip-hop routine that shook the stage and rocked the audience—who leaped to their feet to dance in the aisles!

The house lights came up, revealing an audience hooked on Cheetah power and movin' to their beat. Chanel spied Marisol among them, dancing to the contagious rhythm.

Chanel grabbed the mike. "When we came to Spain, we never expected to find growl power in full effect, but we did, and it's here tonight . . . *esta noche!*"

Chanel's eyes danced as they connected with Marisol's. "We want to bring up our friend, our *amiga* Cheetah *por siempre* . . . Barcelona's own Marisol!"

The light followed Chanel's gesture, finding Marisol. "Come on up!" Chuchie cried. "*Viene!*"

The theater went wild. Marisol made her way through the crowd and onto the stage. To everyone's amazement, she jumped into the act as if she were another Cheetah Girl.

Joaquin and some of his fellow students joined the girls onstage for a final dance number. And the girls finished their performance to off-the-hook cheers and applause.

It didn't take long for the judges to pass their ballots to the announcer. The man studied the notes in front of him, then stepped up to the microphone.

"Congratulations to the festival winners, the Cheetah Girls!"

The girls walked out from the wings and took their bows, pulling Marisol, Angel, and Joaquin out with them. In the audience, Dorothea, Juanita, and Luc clapped louder than anyone.

Onstage, Galleria, Chanel, Aqua, and

Dorinda joined hands with the others on the stage.

Four girls, one dream, Galleria thought. *Amigas* Cheetahs—friends forever!